FOLK TALES
FROM AROUND THE WORLD

Tales of Challenge

S0-CRS-927

STECK-VAUGHN
LITERATURE LIBRARY

This book is dedicated to all folk tale collectors
and storytellers of the past, present, and future,
without whom these stories would be lost.

Project Editor: Anne Rose Souby
Cover Designer: D. Childress

Product Development and Design: Kirchoff/Wohlberg, Inc.

Editorial Director: Mary Jane Martin
Managing Editor: Nancy Pernick
Project Director: Alice Boynton
Graphic Designer: Richarda Hellner

The credits and acknowledgments that appear on page 80
are hereby made a part of this copyright page.

Copyright © 1990 National Education Corporation.
All rights reserved. No part of the material protected by this copyright
may be reproduced or utilized in any form or by any means, electronic or
mechanical, including photocopying, recording, or by any information
storage and retrieval system, without permission in writing from the
copyright owner. Requests for permission to make copies of any part
of the work should be mailed to: Copyright Permissions,
Steck-Vaughn Company, P.O. Box 26015, Austin, Texas 78755.

Library of Congress Cataloging-in-Publication Data
Tales of challenge.
p.   cm.—(Folk tales from around the world)
Summary: An anthology of seven folk tales describing
challenging situations and glorious triumphs.
ISBN 0-8114-2403-0 (lib. bdg.)
ISBN 0-8114-4153-9 (pbk.)
1. Tales. [1. Folklore.] I. Steck-Vaughn Company.
II. Series: Folk tales from around the world (Austin, Tex.)
PZ8.1.T145   1990
398.2—dc20   89-11503   CIP   AC

Printed in the United States of America.

3   4   5   6   7   8   9   0   UN   93   92

Steck-Vaughn Literature Library
Folk Tales From Around the World

ANIMAL TALES
HUMOROUS TALES
TALL TALES
TALES OF THE WISE AND FOOLISH
TALES OF WONDER
TALES OF TRICKERY
TALES OF THE HEART
TALES OF JUSTICE
TALES OF NATURE
TALES OF CHALLENGE

Program Consultants

Frances Bennie, Ed.D.
Principal
Wescove School
West Covina, California

Barbara Coulter, Ed.D.
Director
Department of Communication Arts
Detroit Public Schools
Detroit, Michigan

Renee Levitt
Educational Consultant
Scarsdale, New York

Louise Matteoni, Ph.D.
Professor of Education
Brooklyn College
City University of New York
New York, New York

CONTENTS

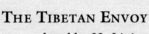

JOHN HENRY

BY ANNE MALCOLMSON

After the Civil War, people began to travel west. They needed railroads to take them across America. Men faced the challenge of laying down thousands of miles of steel railroad track.

John Henry was a real man who worked on the railroad. In time he became a folk tale hero who was larger than life. In stories, he could do the impossible with his strong arms and his hammer.

J OHN Henry, the steel-drivin' man, was as big as an oak and as strong as a bull. As a baby, he sat on his old pappy's knee in East Virginny. And his old pappy said to him, "John Henry, my son, you're gonna be a steel-drivin' man."

The little boy smiled up into his pappy's eyes and nodded. Then he looked ahead into the Years to Come and said, "The Big Bend Tunnel on the C. & O. Railroad is gonna be the end of me."

The Civil War was fought. The slaves were set free. The United States began to grow, spreading from the Atlantic to the Pacific. Everywhere men were chopping down trees, clearing farms, digging ditches, blasting tunnels, and building houses, farms, factories, bridges, railroads— trying to make room for themselves.

In spite of the prophecy, John Henry went to work for the railroads when he grew up. On one of his early jobs he belonged to a crew which laid the track. They had still a hundred yards to finish when the foreman looked into the valley and saw the 5:15 express heading for them sixty miles an hour. The sun was shining in the engineer's eyes. He failed to see the flags signaling him to stop. In another ten minutes that express train would hit the unfinished track. There was going to be an awful wreck. The foreman waved his arms and yelled. But the 5:15 kept on coming lickety-split.

Then John Henry came to the rescue. He told the other workmen to stand back out of his way. He wrapped the hundred yards of steel track into a coil. Once, twice, he swung it around his head. On the third swing he let go. As straight as an arrow the track shot out into the air and fell to earth right in its proper place.

There was still no time to lose. John Henry grabbed a mouthful of spikes and picked up a heavy hammer in each hand. He ran down the ties as fast as he could go, spitting out the spikes through his teeth and smashing them into place.

As he drove in the last spike and jumped aside, the 5:15 rushed past without so much as a jolt. Until he got back to the roundhouse and heard the story, the engineer didn't even know what danger his train had escaped.

As a reward for John Henry's heroism the railroad made him a steel-drivin' man on the Big Bend Tunnel. The steel-drivin' men were the brave fellows who blasted the tunnels through the mountains. They drove long rods of steel into the heart of the rock to make holes for the dynamite. The holes had to be deep. It took a strong man to hammer a steel bar into a granite boulder. These tunnelmen were the biggest, toughest, strongest workmen in the world.

Of them all, John Henry proved to be the biggest, toughest, and strongest. With each hammer stroke he could drive the steel twice as far into the rock as the next man. He could strike twice as fast, too. He worked so fast that his helper, Li'l Bill, had to have a bucket of ice water on hand to keep the handles of his sledges from catching fire. Even so, the big steel-driver burned up two hammers a day. Cap'n Tommy, his boss, said proudly that John Henry did the work of four men. He loved him as he loved his own son.

One day a stranger came to the tunnel selling a

new-fangled gadget. It was a steam drill. He said it could drill holes faster than three men working together.

"That's nothing," said Cap'n Tommy. "You can take your engine and get out. I've a steel-drivin' man, name of John Henry, who can drill holes faster than four men working together."

The salesman, who didn't know any better, laughed politely.

"Don't waste your time and mine, sir," added Cap'n Tommy. "My man can beat your drill to the

bottom of a spike any day in the week. Good day, sir."

The salesman did not leave. He tried a new approach. "I'll tell you what I'll do, Cap'n," he said. "I'll make a little bet with you. If your man can beat my drill, you may have the drill free, absolutely free. If he can't do it, you buy two drills from me. That ought to be fair enough."

That touched the Cap'n's pride. He went around to see John Henry.

"There's a man in town who says his steam drill can beat you driving steel, son. That isn't so, is it?" he asked.

"Of course not," laughed John Henry. "You bring that thing around here and I'll show him."

Polly Ann, John Henry's pretty wife, overheard the conversation. She remembered the prophecy that John Henry had spoken when he was a baby on his pappy's knee. "Big Bend Tunnel on the C. & O. Railroad is gonna be the end of me." She begged him not to try.

John Henry only laughed. "I'm a steel-drivin' man. I'll beat this steam drill if I lay down my hammer and die doin' it," he said.

Cap'n Tommy slapped John Henry on the back for joy. The bet was made. The tunnel crew prepared for the contest. John Henry bought a fine new hammer with a twelve-pound head and a four-foot handle. He named it Polly Ann for good luck.

At last the great morning arrived. People came from the mountains of Pennsylvania and Virginia and Kentucky to see John Henry race the drill. Polly Ann, in her best blue dress, brought her little baby and laid him in the grass where he could see his pappy. John Henry took up his position. Li'l Bill brought the bucket of ice water and stood ready to hold the spike in place.

Cap'n Tommy, in his high silk hat, made a speech to the crowd. At its end he turned to John Henry. "Son," he said, "if you beat that contraption, I'll give you fifty dollars and a new suit."

The onlookers shouted, "John Henry, you can't beat that drill."

"Who says I can't?" called back the giant, rubbing his hands together. "Why, I'll drive my steel into the rock before it gets started."

Then the timekeeper fired his gun and the race began. Slowly at first, then more quickly the heavy sledges fell. *Chug-chug-chug*, the steam drill drove its spike inch by inch into the rock. *Bom-bom-bom*, John Henry drove his. The only sound in all the mountains was the rhythm of the blows.

The water in Li'l Bill's bucket was soon hissing with steam. The steady thunder of the hammers

made some of the country people fear that the mountains themselves were falling down. At the end of the first hour the steam drill was forging ahead. For every *bom-bom,* there came a *chug-chug-chug.*

"Pour some water over me," called John Henry. So Polly Ann poured spring water over his back to wash off the dust. All the while she was doing it he kept on driving, faster, faster, faster.

At the end of the second hour the *bom-chug, bom-chug, bom-chug* sounded like a hurricane. John Henry had caught up with the drill. The muscles rippled under his black skin. The sweat ran in rivers off his nose and his back.

"Li'l Bill, sing to me—and sing fast," said John Henry. So Li'l Bill sang his favorite hammer song. John Henry kept time.

Now, in the third hour, he pulled ahead. For every two *chugs* came three *boms.* His spike was going deeper than the drill's. The veins stood out on his temples. His dark blue dungarees were drenched black with sweat. Bill kept on singing and John Henry kept swinging.

And then the crowd began to cheer. John Henry had six inches more to go, the steam drill had a foot. *Bom-bom-bom!* Three inches! *Bom-bom-bom!* Two inches, one inch!

Cap'n Tommy clapped his hands. Polly Ann cried. The mountains echoed with the cheering of the onlookers. John Henry had won! The steam drill had still eight inches to go. Like a great shrieking tornado, the crowd rushed forward to clasp the hero's hand. But they stopped suddenly, in silence.

For there beside his spike lay John Henry, gasping for breath. He'd won, all right. He'd beaten the drill. But with his last powerful stroke, his great heart had burst within him. Polly Ann knelt beside him and placed his little baby in the palm of his hand.

John Henry looked down at the baby, just as his own pappy had looked down at him. John Henry said, "Son, you're gonna be a steel-drivin' man. But the Big Bend Tunnel is the end of me."

And with that John Henry laid down his hammer and he died.

THE MIDGET AND THE GIANT

BY LEE COOPER

Giants are favorite characters in folk tales. In many stories, these big bullies enjoy making threats and frightening people. Usually there is one person brave enough to face the giant and destroy his power. Jack, in the well-known story "Jack the Giant Killer," is one such hero.

This tale is from France. In it, a giant is amazed when his strength is challenged by a man who stands only four feet high.

PIPÊTE was only four feet tall and everyone in the village, the cheesemaker, the tailor, the hunter, *everyone*, liked to tease him about it. Even the mayor joined in the fun.

"You know why Pipête laughs when he walks across a lawn?" the mayor joked. "He's so short the grass tickles him under his arms!"

Now Pipête didn't like being laughed at, but there was nothing he could do about it. He just grinned uncomfortably and promised himself that *some day* the people in this village would look up to him, even if he had to climb a mountain to make them do it!

And that's just about what happened.

One day he walked into the village and saw all the townspeople crowding around a poor shepherd who was lying on the street. The shepherd's clothes were torn and he was battered and bruised.

Everyone looked scared. The women were all crying loudly. The mayor's mouth was twitching nervously.

"What happened?" asked Pipête.

The women cried louder.

The mayor opened his mouth and these words finally came out, "Monsieur Ropotou has come b-b-back!"

Now these words, though they caused everyone else to cringe with horror, affected Pipête not
at all.

"You are too young to know what this means!"
explained the mayor. "But we remember very
well when he was here before! No one was al-
lowed out of the village, even to hunt or to graze
their herds. We were all his prisoners!"

"And also his victims!" cried the hunter whose
falcon was perched on his shoulder. "Monsieur
Ropotou forced me and my horse to jump over a
cliff! My horse was killed and both my legs were
broken!"

Pipête now understood why everyone was so
concerned.

"And that's not all!" cried the cheesemaker.
"My father's herd was starving so he took them

up on the slope to graze. But Monsieur Ropotou slew every one of them and threw my father down the side of the mountain just the way he did this poor shepherd!"

The women started wailing again as they looked at the suffering shepherd still lying in the street.

Now with all this crying and wailing and agonizing, Pipête was beginning to become very impatient.

"Then let's do something about this Ropotou!" he exclaimed. "Why should we let one man terrorize an entire village?"

"But, Pipête, you don't understand," cried the tailor. "Monsieur Ropotou is not a man, he is a *giant!*"

And that was the truth. He was as tall as a tree, as big as a boulder, as tough as a tornado. He made all the villagers look like midgets. They didn't like it but they could do no more about it than Pipête could about being only four feet tall.

"But we must do something!" said Pipête.

"There's nothing we can do," declared the mayor sadly. "We'll just have to stay quietly in the village and hope he goes away before our herds starve to death!"

But at this moment the wounded shepherd

spoke to them in a low, quivering voice, "This time he will not go away! He said that he is going to destroy the village!"

With this announcement two of the women fainted, the rest renewed their wailing and the men looked at each other in despair.

"What are we going to do?" they asked the mayor.

But before the mayor could answer, they heard the crash of falling timber. They looked up. The giant had pushed aside two trees and was stepping out of the forest. He put his hands on his hips and stared arrogantly down at the villagers.

Their fear was matched only by the shock they felt when Pipête, the midget of the village, called up to the giant, "You are not strong enough to destroy this village!"

"WHAT?" roared the giant, so loudly that the leaves blew off the nearest trees.

Pipête shouted out again, "You're not strong enough to destroy this village!"

The giant had never been talked to like that before in his long, long life!

He bellowed, "WHO IS THAT SO FOOLISH AS TO CHALLENGE A GIANT?"

Pipête stepped to one side so the giant could see him.

"*I* challenge you!" he cried. "Wait there and I'll prove that you are not so strong!"

The villagers whispered to each other that Pipête was sacrificing himself to spare the village just a few minutes longer.

"Is there anything we can do for you?" they asked.

"Yes," said Pipête. And he asked the cheese-maker for some white cheese, which he rolled into a ball and placed in his right pocket.

Then he asked the tailor for a spool of strong thread. He put the thread in his left pocket.

And finally he asked the hunter for his falcon.

He smoothed down the feathers and placed the bird in his back pocket. Then he shook hands with the mayor and left the village.

Everyone watched as he climbed the slope. He seemed to get smaller and smaller as he approached the giant.

Monsieur Ropotou looked down, down at Pipête.

"SO," he thundered. "*YOU* ARE THE ONE WHO CHALLENGED MY STRENGTH!"

Pipête put his hands on his hips and looked up, up at the giant.

"Yes," he replied in a small voice.

"AND I SUPPOSE THAT YOU THINK *YOU* ARE AS STRONG AS *I* AM!" the giant roared.

"I think that I am *stronger* than you are!" Pipête replied calmly.

"YOU...? STRONGER THAN *I*...?" sputtered the giant. "WE'LL SEE ABOUT THAT!"

The giant picked up a medium-sized stone.

"SEE THIS STONE?" he said. "WATCH WHAT HAPPENS WHEN IT HITS THAT ELM TREE."

And the giant hurled the stone. It hit the trunk of the tree and shattered into three pieces.

The villagers watched, too.

"Oh-h-h-h!" they exclaimed.

Then Pipête picked up a similar stone. He pointed to another tree and said, "Watch what happens when it hits that oak tree!"

When the giant turned to look at the tree, Pipête dropped the stone and reached into his right pocket for the ball of white cheese. He threw the cheese as hard as he could at the trunk of the tree. When it hit, it scattered into ninety-three pieces.

The villagers cried, "Bravo, Pipête!" and the giant blinked in amazement. But then he picked up another stone and said, "WELL, PERHAPS YOU CAN THROW HARDER THAN I CAN, BUT NO ONE CAN THROW *HIGHER!*"

And he hurled the stone high, high into the air. It went up, up and kept on going up. It almost touched a cloud!

The giant stepped back proudly.

"NOW IT'S YOUR TURN," he said.

Pipête stooped down and selected a gray, oblong stone. But as he drew his arm back for his throw, he skillfully let the stone fall behind him and seized the falcon that was in his back pocket. He tossed the falcon straight up in the air.

The falcon looked for all the world like the gray stone. But unlike a stone, it didn't fall back to the earth. It went up, up and kept on going up. It touched the cloud! It went *through* the cloud and kept going as far as the eye could see.

"HOOP-LA!" the giant exclaimed. He was amazed and shaken.

But not wishing to lose a contest with a midget, he walked over to a huge oak tree, wrapped his thick arms around the trunk and rocked the tree back and forth. Then, with a mighty tug, he wrenched the roots right out of the ground. The uprooted tree toppled to the ground with a mighty CRASH!

The villagers saw this with dismay. How could Pipête possibly match this feat! Why, his little arms would hardly reach around a pine sapling!

But Pipête didn't hesitate for a moment. He took the spool of thread out of his left pocket and with great confidence tied one end of it securely around the trunk of a tree. Then he ran in a wide circle around the giant, encircling him in the middle of about fifty huge trees.

It looked as if Pipête could, just by pulling the string a little bit tighter, uproot all fifty trees, making them crash right on top of the giant!

"STOP! STOP!" cried the giant. "YOU WIN! I

CAN SEE THAT YOU ARE STRONGER THAN I.
IF YOU WILL JUST LET ME GO, I WILL LEAVE
THIS COUNTRY FOREVER!"

So Pipête rolled the string back on the spool,
said good-bye to the giant and returned to the
village.

The townspeople carried him down the streets
on their shoulders, cheering happily. The mayor
asked him to take over his office but Pipête
refused.

"It just wouldn't look right for the leader of the
village to be so short," he declared.

"Pshaw!" the mayor replied, handing Pipête
his staff of authority. "The level of your thinking
is much more important than the level of your
eyebrows!"

So Pipête, being a high-minded citizen, accepted the office. And the villagers have looked
up to him ever since.

THE CHIEF'S RIDDLE

BY VIVIAN L. THOMPSON

Hawaii was once ruled by mighty chiefs. They held the power of life and death over their people. Their people knew that it was best not to anger them.

In many Hawaiian tales, the characters did what people did not dare to do in real life. They had contests with the chief. In this folk story, skill in sports and in answering riddles is needed. Winning can bring great rewards. Losing can mean death.

ONCE in the section of Oahu called Moana-lua, there lived a chief who was most vain. Whenever he appeared before his people, he watched to make sure that he was the center of attention.

One day he noticed an odd thing. His men all bowed low to the ground when he passed, but the women—especially the young women—stole glances from the corners of their eyes, at someone behind him. Turning, he saw that it was Mekila the handsome, a fine young warrior in his train, to whom their eyes were drawn.

The chief was torn with jealousy and searched for a way to discredit his handsome young rival. Being known as an expert bowler, the chief challenged Mekila to a game of maika.

Mekila accepted. What else could he do?

The people gathered at the course to watch. The chief took his disc of black lava rock and sent it bowling a distance of thirty yards. The watchers clapped.

Mekila took his disc of white sandstone and sent it bowling a distance of forty yards. The watchers clapped and cheered. The chief congratulated Mekila briefly, and withdrew.

Next day the chief, an expert at sledding, challenged Mekila to a contest with the holua sled.

Mekila accepted. What choice had he?

The crowd followed to the steep holua course. An attendant carried the chief's favorite holua sled made of highly-polished mamane wood, its runners gleaming with kukui nut oil. Mekila followed, carrying his own simple sled of uhi-uhi wood.

When all eyes were upon him, the chief picked up his sled, ran with it, and cast himself down. He flew over the course, traveling one hundred and fifty yards before he came to rest. The watchers shouted.

Mekila, on his sled, traveled one hundred and seventy yards. The watchers shouted and whistled. The chief congratulated Mekila coldly, and withdrew.

On the third day the chief, an expert surfer, challenged Mekila to a surfing contest. Mekila accepted.

All gathered at the beach to watch. The chief took his ten-foot board of glossy wili-wili wood, pushed it out into the sea and waited for a towering wave. He caught it, rose gracefully to his feet, and rode the wave straight in to shallow water. The watchers cheered.

Mekila took his well-worn seven-foot board of koa wood, caught a slanting wave and rode it twice the distance, landing in the shallows far down the beach. The watchers cheered and shouted, "Hana hou! Do it again!"

This time the chief did not wait to congratulate Mekila but stalked off angrily. How was he to get rid of this skillful young rival? There were no other fields in which the chief himself was expert. What should he do now? It was a riddle. . . .

A riddle! That was the answer. Riddling was a chiefly accomplishment. It was unlikely that Mekila had received any training in the art. Aia la! That was it!

But auwe! The chief himself was no riddler, having neither the time nor patience for it. Ah, but there was that wise man Paeli living in the mountains of Moana-lua. He could provide a tricky riddle!

The chief paid him a visit. Next day, he challenged Mekila to a riddling contest.

This time, Mekila hesitated. "O Chief, I know nothing of the art of riddling . . . but if it is your wish, I will try."

"It is my wish," the chief replied curtly. "Here is the riddle:

In the morning, four legs.
At noon, two legs.
At evening, three legs.

"You have a week to find the answer. If you fail, death in the earth oven."

The watchers stood silent. The chief had not stated the terms of the contest until after Mekila had accepted the challenge. They knew now that the chief sought not a fair contest but a sure way to take Mekila's life. It was unjust but what could be done about it?

They could not defy their chief. They could not help Mekila find the answer.

Mekila set out bravely upon his quest. He traveled the length and breadth of the district. Of everyone he met he asked the same question, "What has four legs at morning, two legs at noon, three legs at evening?" None could answer.

Mekila studied the people he met. No answer. He studied the animals—the pig, dog, and rat. He studied the birds, the insects. Still no answer.

His time was nearly gone. On the morrow he must admit defeat and go to his death in the earth oven. Mekila started home. As he traveled the mountain path through Moana-lua he came upon old Paeli playing with his grandson.

"Have you found the answer?" Paeli asked.

Mekila shook his head wearily.

"Then hear me," said Paeli. "When you approach the chief, take care, for he seeks your life. I cannot give you the answer but this much I will tell you. The chief found his riddle here and here

you will find the
answer, if you give
the matter careful
thought. I can say no
more." He called his
grandson, waved to
Mekila, then leaning on his cane, hobbled off.

Mekila started on his way, walking slowly, lost
in thought. What had Paeli meant? There had
been three persons in the group . . . and the riddle
had three parts. He repeated the lines again and
laughed aloud. Now he knew the answer!

On the following day as Mekila left his home,

he saw crowds gathering. He saw too, his fellow warriors lined up in ranks before the chief's house. He could guess what their orders were. If he was to see another sun, he must find a way to answer the chief and still avoid his warriors.

Desperately Mekila looked about. Opposite the chief's house stood a tall, flat-topped hill. Children were playing there now, waiting for the contest to begin. Mekila started toward them.

The chief's crier began his circle of the village. "Everyone is summoned to the chief's house for the riddling contest. Today Mekila must answer the chief's riddle or roast in the earth oven!"

A cloud of steam was already rising from the imu. The crier returned. There was no sign of Mekila.

"Sound the shell trumpet four times!" the chief ordered. "If Mekila does not come forth, my warriors shall find him and drag him to the imu!"

The conch shell sounded its low, sad call . . . once . . . twice . . . three times . . . . No sign of Mekila. It sounded its fourth and final summons. Before the echo died away, a shout came from the hilltop across from the chief's house. There stood Mekila.

"I have brought you an answer, O Chief," he called.

Then before the chief's startled eyes, Mekila began to act out the riddle's answer. He showed the sun coming up, and an infant crawling on all fours. He showed the sun high overhead, and a young man walking straight and tall. He showed the sun going down, and an old man hobbling on a cane.

The people gave a glad shout, and no one shouted louder than Mekila's fellow warriors. The vain chief, hearing the sound, knew that he had best make no further plans against Mekila's life. He had been outwitted by the riddler on the hill.

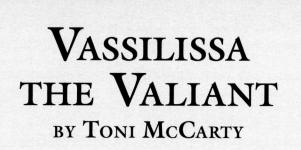

VASSILISSA
THE VALIANT

BY TONI MCCARTY

Long ago, Russia was ruled by kings called *tsars*. Russians loved to tell stories in which the tsar and his generals, the grand dukes, were outwitted.

This story is about Vassilissa. She is a heroine who appears in many Russian folk tales. Vassilissa is not only brave. She is also clever, skilled, and very beautiful. Vassilissa stands ready and able to meet even the most unusual challenge.

THE Grand Duke Vladimir of Kiev was a proud man. He enjoyed inviting the princes of the land to feast in his castle, where he could show off his riches.

But one night, a young prince named Staver grew bored with Vladimir's boasting. Turning to Pavel, the prince next to him, Staver said, "Really, what the Duke owns is not so special. My own castle is so big that I ride horseback through its halls. I love the ringing sound of my horse's golden shoes on the floor." Staver plucked a loud chord on the strings of his gusla. "My greatest treasure, by far, is Vassilissa, my beautiful and

brave wife. She has eyes bright as an eagle's, and a face as smooth as snow. But her true beauty is her skill." Staver leaned over and whispered to Pavel, "In a contest, she can outdo any man."

Staver's words spread quickly around the Grand Duke's table. When Duke Vladimir heard what Staver had said, he rose and like a wild boar bellowed, "Enough! How dare this Staver brag in my castle. Put him in chains, drag him down to the dungeon, and pile the sands high in front of his cell so that he may never escape. Then go to his wretched castle and bring me this woman Vassilissa!" The Duke's men seized Staver roughly. The gusla slipped from his hands and clattered to the floor.

As Staver was being locked in chains, Pavel slipped quietly away. He hurried to Vassilissa and warned her that Duke Vladimir's men were coming to get her.

Quickly, Vassilissa dressed herself in men's clothing, tucked her hair under her hat, and pulled on riding boots of green morocco leather. She slung a quiver of arrows across her back and grabbed her bow and Tartar sword. With twelve horsemen behind her dressed as Tartars, she rode off toward the castle of Duke Vladimir.

On the way, they came upon the Duke's men.

"We're going to the castle
of Staver," the Duke's
men said, "to capture his
wife Vassilissa. Who are
you, young man?"

"I am the messenger of the Great Tartar Khan,"
said Vassilissa. "Your Grand Duke Vladimir owes
the Khan twelve years' tribute in gold. The Khan

is angry. He's tired of waiting for his gold, and we've come for it now."

The Duke's men were frightened. They knew the power of the Tartar Khan was far greater than Vladimir's.

Vassilissa continued. "As for this Vassilissa you seek, you've lost her. When we stopped there, seeking refreshment, her castle was deserted. She must be miles away by now."

The Duke's men galloped back to the castle of Vladimir to report the news.

"Vassilissa has escaped," they told him. "But far worse, the Tartar Khan has sent his men to collect twelve years of tribute in gold. They're almost at your gate."

When Vassilissa arrived with her twelve men, she saw the tables had been hurriedly set. She smiled to herself; how anxious Vladimir was to please the messenger of the Tartar Khan! She knew he could never come up with as much gold as she was demanding.

After greeting Vassilissa and bidding her welcome, Vladimir felt a tug on his sleeve. His wife Apraksiya pulled him aside. "That so-called messenger of the Khan is not a man at all," she said. "She glides across the courtyard with the grace of a ship on the waters. That's a woman, Vladimir."

"We'll soon see about that," said the Duke, raising his eyebrows. Perhaps his wife was right. In a hearty voice, Vladimir proposed a contest in wrestling.

Vassilissa bowed her head in agreement. She threw the first man to the ground so violently that he had to be carried away. She knocked a second off his feet before he knew what was happening. Vassilissa flipped a third man on his head and knocked him out cold.

Duke Vladimir scowled at his wife. "How could a woman beat three strong men! Don't make a fool of me."

But Apraksiya was not convinced. "Look again, my Duke. See the skin, smooth as snow, and watch the way that she moves. No man is quite so graceful, you must admit."

The Duke looked closely at Vassilissa. Perhaps Apraksiya was right. The Duke then called for a contest in archery. "The bowmen must pierce that oak in the distance with their arrows," he said. One by one, his best archers took aim and struck the oak. Then Vassilissa took aim. Her arrow flew to the tree and hit it with such force that the oak shuddered and split wide open.

"There!" said Vladimir to Apraksiya. "Are you satisfied now? He is a man's man, indeed."

"Eyes sharp as an eagle's," said Apraksiya, and walked away. The Duke would have given up, but his wife seemed so sure of herself he tried again.

This time the Duke challenged Vassilissa to a game of chess. She beat him three times in a row quite easily, then pushed the board aside.

"Enough playing games. I've come for the gold you owe the Tartar Khan. Let's not waste any more time."

Vladimir frowned and grumbled. "I'm a poor man, sir. I cannot pay the Khan in gold."

"Well, then, what *can* you give the Khan that might please him and make him forget what you owe?" asked Vassilissa.

"Look around my court," said Vladimir. "What would you choose for the Tartar Khan? You know what would please him better than I know."

"Nothing here would catch his fancy. You don't have many musicians. Good heavens! Not even one gusla player. The Khan is so fond of gusla music."

Vladimir's eyes brightened. "The gusla! We *do* have one young prince who plays the gusla beautifully. He sings, as well." The Duke leaped to his feet and ordered his men to fetch Staver right away.

When Staver was brought up from the dungeon to the banquet room, he looked bewildered. Vladimir shoved a gusla in his hands and ordered him to play.

Staver plucked the strings slowly and sadly, his eyes on the floor. Then he raised his head, and his eyes lit upon Vassilissa. He recognized her right away and his heart sang. His songs became so gay and lighthearted that all the people in the Duke's court began dancing.

At last Vassilissa said, "Well . . . I suppose he will do. I'll take him to the Tartar Khan and you may pray that the Khan is satisfied."

Staver mounted his horse and galloped off with Vassilissa.

"How easily I got out of that one," said the Duke. "A gusla player! I was lucky to have had that Staver on hand just when I needed him."

But no one felt luckier than Staver himself as he rode away beside the gallant Vassilissa—she who could beat a man at any game.

THE BOW, THE DEER, AND THE TALKING BIRD

RETOLD BY ANITA BRENNER

The Aztec had lived in Mexico since the 1200s. Over the next two hundred years, they built a very great empire. Then early in the 1500s, Spanish explorers arrived in Mexico. They took over all of Mexico for Spain. But the old Aztec stories lived on.

In this tale, an Aztec merchant gives a bow, a bird, and a deer to his sons. The father says that all three are priceless treasures. See if you agree.

A rich Aztec merchant was dying and he called his three sons and said, "My sons, my time upon this earth is ended. I have tried to be a loyal friend, an honest merchant, and a brave warrior. I have educated you as well as I was able and I hope that if I have any enemies it is more because of their envy than for any wickedness of mine. Besides my advice and example, I wish to leave you three things. If managed properly, they will be better than the greatest riches. These three things are a bow that always sends the arrow true to its aim, a deer that will take his master anywhere he wants to go, and a bird that speaks of what it sees." He died.

The eldest son said, "As I am the eldest, I should have first choice of the inheritance. I choose the bow." For he thought to himself, "With a bow like that I can kill the rarest birds and become a rich trader in fine feathers and plumes."

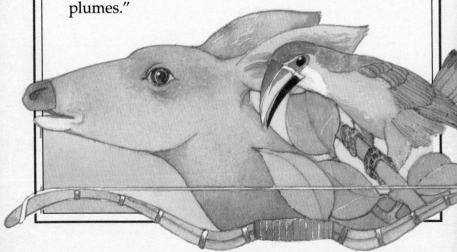

The second son said, "Between a gabby-bird and a deer that will take me anywhere I want to go, I choose the deer."

So the youngest son took what was left: the bird. He thought, "I will take care of it lovingly. There may not be much use in a bird like that but it belonged to my dear father." Then they all went off to seek their fortunes.

Many years later the two oldest brothers heard that the youngest one was now a great and famous man. He was the Prime Minister to the king. His advice and warnings and opinions were listened to, for they were always wise and true. The two brothers became very jealous when they heard this, and they plotted to kill him, steal the bird that they had so thoughtlessly refused, and take their brother's place. They well knew that it was the wonderful bird that had made him Prime Minister.

They did not notice that while they were talking, the very same bird was sitting on a branch above their heads. The bird heard them, and flew to tell the youngest son. Tears came to his eyes. "Alas," he said, "I am not afraid of my brothers. I can take care of myself. I do not think they are really bad at heart. Let us see what can be done."

The next day the two brothers arrived at the

king's court. They pretended to be overcome with surprise and joy at their youngest brother's luck in being such an important man. He received them with tears in his eyes and gave them the best rooms in the palace, and introduced them to the king, too. The brothers went to sleep early, for the eldest was tired from walking so far and the second brother had a sore throat from the dust that his deer had made as it ran swiftly along the roads.

The youngest son sat down as he did every evening to listen to his little bird. The bird perched on his shoulder and said softly, "The

king of the country next to ours has decided to make war on us and conquer us. He wants to take us by surprise. His army will march against us and attack early tomorrow morning. They will take the road that lies below the steep cliff at the mouth of the river." When the bird finished whispering this information into his master's ear, he flew away. But the young man went to the king at once and told him what was going to happen.

"Oh dear, oh dear," said the king. "Our best captains are off on a picnic and the soldiers are having a holiday. What shall we do?"

"Most worthy Sire," said the youngest brother, "if Your Majesty promises to make nobles of my brothers and myself, we three will save you no matter how strong the enemy turns out to be."

"I promise," said the king, but he didn't have much hope. He didn't see how three young men, no matter how brave, could stop all the armies of his powerful neighbor.

The youngest one hurried to his brothers and woke them. "My brothers," he said, "our father was such a brave man that still today, people say when they hear our name, oh, yes, they are the sons of that warrior who never knew what it was to be afraid. Don't you think we are obliged to uphold his reputation and for the honor of our name, go out and defend our native land?" Then he explained what was going to happen. And he made plans.

"Your little deer," said he to the middle brother, "will take us to the cliff quickly, in plenty of time, because what army can travel as fast and far as a deer? Then when we get there my bird will tell us exactly where the enemy is hiding. And you with your bow," he said to the eldest brother, "can do the shooting."

The three brothers climbed on the deer's back, and the small bird perched on the youngest one's shoulder. The middle brother said, "Quickly, quickly, little deer," and in less than a minute, even less than a second, they were at the cliff. They hid in some bushes and the bird went off on a scouting trip, to see what he could see. He came back quickly and told them where the enemy was hidden, and exactly where the king of the attacking soldiers was.

The eldest brother fitted an arrow to his bow, aimed where the little bird told him, and shot. The arrow traveled far away where the wicked king was hiding, whang! through his heart. The army was frightened and bewildered. The soldiers said, "This is very strange, let us go home." But one captain, bolder than the others, jumped up and shouted, "Forward, my brave boys, let us avenge the death of our great and noble king!" The eldest brother fitted another arrow to his bow, aimed at the captain, and the arrow traveled far and fast, whang! And the captain fell dead.

The soldiers began to run back to their own country as fast as they could. By the time the sun rose they were all gone, running, some on galloping horses, some on foot. The three brothers put the dead king and the dead captain on the deer's back, and they all went home to breakfast.

The people came out to meet them, singing and dancing and cheering. The king made nobles of the three brothers and gave them rich presents, lands, houses, horses, wonderful things. They lived happily after that because they had found out something important: that together they could do more than separately, and that there is nothing better than a good brother. Ever since then, when people know a secret, they say, "Oh, a little bird told me."

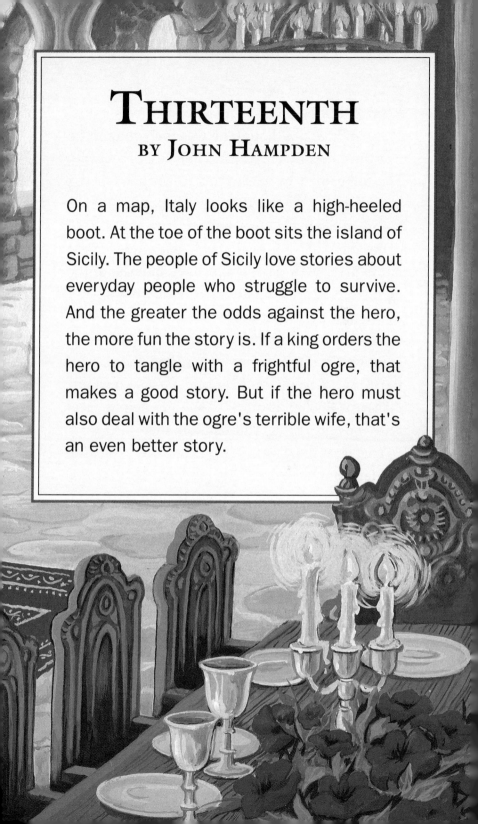

THIRTEENTH

BY JOHN HAMPDEN

On a map, Italy looks like a high-heeled boot. At the toe of the boot sits the island of Sicily. The people of Sicily love stories about everyday people who struggle to survive. And the greater the odds against the hero, the more fun the story is. If a king orders the hero to tangle with a frightful ogre, that makes a good story. But if the hero must also deal with the ogre's terrible wife, that's an even better story.

I N Sicily long ago there was a poor man who had thirteen sons. The youngest was called Thirteenth, and although he was the youngest he was the tallest, strongest, and quickest of them all. The father had to work hard to support such a large family, but he did his best by gathering herbs, and all his sons helped. The mother, to make the children quick, said that whoever got home first every day should have the best of the herb soup. Thirteenth always got home first, and this made the other brothers so cross that they were always grumbling about it in the village.

Presently these grumbles reached the ears of the King of Sicily, and he said to his courtiers, "Perhaps this lad is quick enough to help us deal with the ogre. Bring Thirteenth to me."

This ogre lived with his ogress wife in a castle not far from the palace. He was very ugly, strong, and greedy, always robbing people and even sometimes eating them, and everybody was afraid of him.

When Thirteenth appeared, the King said, "Now, you must go and steal the coverlet from the ogre's bed while he is asleep. That will be a lesson for him and I will give you a bag of gold."

"Your Majesty," cried Thirteenth, "how can I? If the ogre sees me, he will eat me."

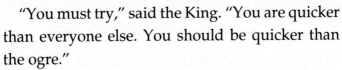

"You must try," said the King. "You are quicker than everyone else. You should be quicker than the ogre."

Thirteenth went off reluctantly to the ogre's castle and waited behind the bushes outside until he saw the ogre go out hunting and the ogress go into the kitchen to cook supper. Then Thirteenth slipped quietly into the castle, stole upstairs, and hid under the ogre's bed. When the ogre came up to his bedroom that night, he said, "I smell the smell of a human! I will eat him up!" Thirteenth shivered with fright, but the ogress said, "Nonsense! No human has been near the castle all day!"

So they got into bed and were soon fast asleep.

When he heard the ogre snoring, Thirteenth gave a gentle pull at the coverlet to work it loose. The ogre wakened and roared out, "What's that?"

"Miaow! miaow!" said Thirteenth.

"It's only the cat," said the ogress. "Scat! Scat!" she called, clapping her hands.

Soon they were both snoring again.

Thirteenth crawled out, snatched the coverlet, and ran for his life. The ogre was after him in a flash. "I see you, Thirteenth! I'll catch you! I'll eat you!" he howled. But Thirteenth was too quick for him and soon reached the palace, while the ogre was left puffing and gasping far behind.

What rejoicing there was in the poor man's cottage when Thirteenth came home jingling a bag full of golden ducats! His brothers didn't grumble about him then. They all had a great feast and lived together happily, until the King sent for Thirteenth again.

"Now," said the King, "you must go and steal the ogre's horse. Then he will not be able to ride about the country robbing people. Bring me the horse and I will give you three bags of gold."

Thirteenth thought hard for a minute. "Your Majesty," he said, "if you will give me a bag of sweet cakes and a silk ladder with hooks at the end of it, I will see what I can do."

Late that night Thirteenth went to the ogre's castle. The gate was shut and barred, but he threw up the hooks until they caught on the top of the gate, and then he climbed the silk ladder and jumped down into the courtyard. Like a shadow, he crept to the stable. The horse whinnied and stamped, but when Thirteenth gave him a sweet cake, he was quiet again. Thirteenth gave him another cake and another and another and another until the horse was very friendly. Then Thirteenth climbed on its back and walked it

quietly into the courtyard. But when he drew the bolts and swung open the gate, the hinges made a tremendous creaking, for they had not been oiled for a hundred years. The ogre wakened in a fury and came tumbling downstairs into the courtyard roaring, "Thirteenth! I see you! I'll eat you!"

Thirteenth was too quick for him. He clapped his heels to the horse's sides and galloped so fast that he had reached the palace before the ogre had puffed as far as the first milestone.

Thirteenth's family had three more bags of gold, and all lived together happily, until the King sent for him again.

"The ogre is still robbing and killing people," said the King. "He must be taken prisoner and brought to me, and you, Thirteenth, are the only man in Sicily quick enough and brave enough to do it."

"But, your Majesty, how can I? A dozen men could not hold him! He will kill me and eat me."

"You must find a way of doing it," answered the King, "and I will give you seven bags of gold."

There was no help for it. Thirteenth had to sit and think until he had thought of a plan. He got the King's carpenters to make a large strong chest with heavy iron hinges and bolts, and he loaded this on a little cart. He put on a gray beard and a gray wig, he dressed himself as a monk, and he trundled the little cart all the way to the ogre's castle.

"Mr. Ogre," he called, pulling at the bellrope. "Mr. Ogre!"

Very soon the ogre came to the gate to see what all the noise was about.

"Mr. Ogre," said the monk, speaking like an old man. "Does Thirteenth live here?"

"I wish he did," roared the ogre. "I'd break his neck. What do you want him for?"

"He has killed our abbot," said the monk. "I want to capture him and have him punished. But I don't know him. Do you?"

"Know him!" roared the ogre. "I do! I do!"

"How tall is he?" asked the monk.

"As tall as I am."

"When I've captured him," said the monk, "would this chest hold him?"

"I think so," answered the ogre.

"Well, if you're as tall as he is, will you get into the chest so that we can see?"

"I will," said the ogre. "Anything to help catch that rascal!" He climbed into the chest and lay down. "There, you can see it's a good fit."

"Let me try the lid," said Thirteenth, shutting it and shooting the bolts. "Now, can you get out?"

The ogre struggled with all his might, but he could not break out.

"Splendid," said the lad in his own voice. "I am Thirteenth and I am taking you to the King."

The ogre howled and kicked and thumped his hardest, but it was no use. Thirteenth trundled the cart to the palace. The King threw the ogre into the palace dungeon, and put the ogress in with him, and they never killed or ate anyone again.

Then Thirteenth went home, jingling his seven bags full of ducats, and for the rest of their lives he and his family always had enough to eat.

THE TIBETAN ENVOY

TRANSLATED BY HE LIYI

This tale from Tibet is based on a true story of a Chinese princess and a Tibetan prince.

According to the tale, the prince wanted to marry the Chinese princess. First, he needed her father's permission. The prince sent his envoy to speak to the Chinese emperor for him. But at the Chinese palace, there were envoys from six other kingdoms. They all faced the same challenge. Which of them would succeed and win the princess?

MANY years ago, the emperor of the Tang dynasty had a most beloved daughter, the Princess Wencheng. When she was old enough to get married, all the neighboring princes sent an envoy to the capital to propose. And the prince of faraway Tibet also sent an envoy: the wisest man in Tibet, and the most cunning.

There were seven envoys in all. All of them had the same aim, to win Princess Wencheng's love, but all were in doubt. Who would succeed? Nobody knew.

The emperor thought Tibet was too far away. It would be hard to visit his daughter there. He had no mind to let his daughter marry a Tibetan prince, though he could not refuse the Tibetan envoy openly. He held a meeting of his ministers to consider how to reject the Tibetan prince's suit. They decided to set a hard marriage test. When the Tibetan envoy failed, perhaps he would go away and leave them to choose the princess a husband from among the neighboring princes.

On the following day, five hundred mares and their foals were brought to the city square. The foals were driven into the center of the square, and their mothers were tied up round the edge. Then the king declared, "All seven of the princes are as dear and useful to me as my hands and

arms. I really wish I had seven princesses for them. Too bad. I have only one daughter. I don't know whom I should choose. So to be fair, I've brought five hundred mares and their foals here. Now you seven envoys, get busy matching up the mothers and their young. Then I'll consider the marriage."

The seven envoys began. The six local ones rushed about, each trying to lead the foals to the mares, but the Tibetan envoy just waited politely for them to finish. Every time the envoys led a foal to the mares, all the horses bucked and kicked and made a tremendous commotion. The foals were afraid to go near. None of the envoys could match up mare and foal.

At last the Tibetan envoy's turn came. The Tibetans are very experienced with horses; they know just about everything about them. So he didn't blunder around like the others. Instead he asked for food of the best quality to be brought to the mares. All the mares stopped kicking and ate peacefully till they couldn't eat any more. As soon as they were finished, they looked up and neighed loudly. That was a call for the foals to suckle. And the foals all ran to their own mother, all sucking, prancing, licking, or happily whisking their tails.

The emperor appreciated this envoy's quick wits very much, but he still didn't want him to win. So he announced another test. "This envoy is really very clever, and I like him too, but that's not the end. I want to give you all another chance." He took out a piece of elegant green jade and said to the seven envoys, "This jade is as intricate as it is beautiful. Look carefully at it, and you will find a hole twisting and turning right through it. When one of you hangs this jade on a thread, I will consider the marriage."

The Tibetan envoy let the other six try first, but they all failed hopelessly. They tried all day but none of them could get the thread through. At last the Tibetan envoy was asked to try.

The Tibetan envoy caught an ant and tied the thread to its leg. Then he smeared a little honey on the exit hole of the jade. The ant smelled the honey and very quickly got through the hole with the thread trailing behind. The Tibetan envoy tied the two ends together and passed the jade necklace to the king.

The emperor was very surprised. He had to think of a new test the Tibetan might fail. He said, "We will try another competition, so that each one of you will believe I take you seriously." Then he instructed a carpenter to take a log, and plane and polish the wood until each of the ends looked identical. The log was shown to the envoys, and the king said, "Here is a log. Come and examine it. I want you to make out which end comes from the top of the tree, and which from the bottom. I don't want guesswork. If any of you can explain it correctly, the question of my daughter's marriage will be easily decided."

The six local envoys examined it first. One by one they stared at it, turned it, touched it, measured it, but none could make out which end was which. Finally they asked the Tibetan envoy's opinion.

The Tibetan envoy came from the mountains, so he knew that a tree is heavier nearer the root. He asked them to put the log into the river. It floated with the lighter end ahead, the heavier behind. He easily pointed out which was which.

The emperor was impressed by this very clever solution, but he still did not want to send his daughter so far away. Therefore he called another meeting of his ministers. One of them suggested, "Your Majesty should choose three hundred beautiful girls and dress them in the same clothes as the princess. Stand them in a line. If this envoy can tell her apart from the others, it must be fate. I don't think he can do that. In this way your daughter will remain near you."

The emperor agreed to this, and declared, "To be fair to all the envoys, we must have one last test. I have three hundred girls, all dressed alike. The princess is among them. He who identifies her correctly wins her for his master."

Again the six local envoys tried first. They thought the most beautiful girl ought to be the princess, but she wasn't. All of them pointed out the wrong girl.

Meanwhile the Tibetan envoy was busy around the palace trying to learn about the princess. He had never seen her or heard anything specific about her. He had many friends in the palace. He visited the cart drivers, the serving men, and the washerwomen, hoping to find out about the emperor's daughter. At last he met an old washerwoman who knew about the girl, but told him, "I am afraid to tell you anything. Our king has a private magician who knows all secrets. He would find me out and I should die."

The Tibetan calmed her fears. "Madam, you may rely on me. Tell me all you know about her. Do as I say and no magician can find you out." Then he brought three white stones and placed them on the ground. Above the stones he fixed a large iron cauldron filled with water. Then he laid a bench across the cauldron, and sat the

woman on the bench. He gave her a brass trumpet and said, "Speak boldly through this. The wisest magician can only say, 'the speaker lives on a wooden mountain. This wooden mountain is on an iron sea. The sea is at the top of three white mountains. The speaker has a brass mouth.' The emperor can never find you. So, be brave and please tell me all the details you know."

The old woman chuckled at that. She told him without the least fear, "My gentleman, in the first place you must not point at the most beautiful girl. The princess isn't ugly but she is not the most beautiful one. She is a princess, so people usually say she is the nicest girl in the world. Second, don't point at the front row or the back row. That's too obvious. The king puts his daughter in the middle. Third, the princess has worn oil on her hair ever since she was a child. Bees like it, and often fly above her head. She likes the bees, and never waves them away. The other girls have no oil, for the princess gets it from abroad. So if you see bees around her head, you may point at her and she will be just the right princess. That's the gossip among the courtiers. The cooks heard it from them. I washed the cooks' clothes, so I heard it from them. Now, my gentleman, that is all I can tell you. Good luck!"

The Tibetan envoy thanked her and went to make his choice. He was very careful. He didn't point at the back row or the front row, nor at the most beautiful girl. He studied the girls one at a time. At noon, he saw a golden bee dancing above a girl's head. The girl didn't mind the bee. She wasn't afraid of it, but watched it lovingly. The Tibetan envoy pointed straight at her and said, "This is the princess." And it was exactly just the real princess. The emperor and the other six envoys were amazed at his success.

The emperor thought, "This Tibetan envoy has never seen the princess, so how does he know so much more about her than the other envoys? Somebody must have talked to him."

The emperor ordered his magician to find out the culprit. But the magician just talked a lot of nonsense.

The emperor could not help it. He had to say "yes," and allow the Tibetan envoy to talk to the princess face to face.

The Tibetan said to her, "Princess, I am glad to know your father the emperor has promised to let our Tibetan prince marry the best princess on earth. As you are going away with me, the emperor will want to give you a lot of presents. Our Tibetan prince has everything you need. So don't take jewels and silks, but remember what I'm telling you now. Ask him for seeds of all the chief grains. With them we shall make our land fruitful, which is a gift that is more precious than gold and silver."

The princess took his advice. Amazed at his daughter's request, the emperor gave her five hundred horses loaded with grain seeds to take with her to Tibet.

Acknowledgments

Grateful acknowledgment is made to the following authors and publishers for the use of copyrighted materials. Every effort has been made to obtain permission to use previously published material. Any errors or omissions are unintentional.

Blackie and Son Limited for "The Midget and the Giant" from *Five Fables from France* by Lee Cooper. Copyright © 1970 by Lee Cooper.

Delacorte Press, a division of Bantam, Doubleday, Dell Publishing Group, Inc. for "Vassilissa the Valiant" from *The Skull in the Snow and Other Folktales* by Toni McCarty. Copyright © 1981 by Toni McCarty.

Susannah Glusker and Dr. Peter Glusker for "The Bow, the Deer, and the Talking Bird" from *The Boy Who Could Do Anything* by Anita Brenner. Copyright © 1942 and 1970 by Anita Brenner.

Houghton Mifflin Company for "John Henry" from *Yankee Doodle's Cousins* by Anne Malcolmson. Copyright © 1941 by Anne Burnett Malcolmson. Copyright renewed 1969 by Anne Malcolmson von Storch.

Lothrop, Lee and Shepard Books, a division of William Morrow & Co., Inc. for "The Tibetan Envoy" from *The Spring of Butterflies* translated by He Liyi. Text copyright © 1985 by William Collins Sons & Co., Ltd.

Vivian L. Thompson for "Riddler on the Hill" (Retitled: "The Chief's Riddle") from *Hawaiian Legends of Tricksters and Riddlers* by Vivian L. Thompson. Copyright © 1969 by Vivian L. Thompson.

AP Watt Limited on behalf of the Executors of the Estate of John Hampden for "Thirteenth" from *The House of Cats and Other Stories* by John Hampden. Copyright © 1966 by John Hampden.

Illustrations

Frederick Porter: pp. 6-17; Ed Parker: pp. 18-29; Floyd Cooper: pp. 30-39; Alan Nahigian: cover, pp. 40-49; Arvis Stewart: pp. 50-57; Susan Magurn: pp. 58-67; Linda Graves: pp. 68-79.